This book belongs to

_____

Disney

Bambi

The Story of Bambi

Disney

Bambi

The Story of Bambi

PaRragon

Bath · New York · Cologne · Melbourne · Delhi
Hong Kong · Shenzhen · Singapore

This edition published by Parragon Books Ltd in 2016
and distributed by

Parragon Inc.
440 Park Avenue South, 13th Floor
New York, NY 10016
www.parragon.com

ISBN 978-1-4748-5046-9

Printed in China

Flowers sleep
in the winter.

It was a beautiful spring day in the forest.
As the sun rose, the animals woke up to
excited twittering and shouting.

Deep in the forest, Thumper the bunny
was spreading wonderful news.
"A new prince is born!" he shouted.

In a nearby clearing, a mother deer lay with her newborn son.

"This is quite an occasion," said Friend Owl. "It isn't every day a prince is born."

The mother deer named her son Bambi.

Days passed and Bambi began to explore his world, with some help from the friendly forest animals. There was so much to see!

"Good morning," called some opossums hanging from a tree. Bambi turned his head upside down to greet them!

Then a furry creature popped out of
the ground.
"Good morning!" said the mole.
Startled, Bambi tumbled to the ground.
He was still a little unsteady on his feet.

"Get up!" Thumper called out. "Try again!"
Bambi struggled to his feet. He didn't want
to miss any of the fun!

Every day, Bambi's friends showed
him new things.

"Those are birds," they explained.

"Burr!" repeated Bambi.

"It's burr-duh," corrected Thumper.

"Bird! Bird!" said Bambi loudly.
The bunnies cheered.

"Bird!" said Bambi again when
a butterfly landed on his tail.
Thumper laughed. "No, that's
a butterfly!"

Then Thumper introduced his friend
to flowers. But as Bambi bent toward them,
he found himself nose-to-nose with a skunk!

"Flower," said Bambi proudly.
Thumper giggled, but Flower was that little skunk's name from then on. Bambi had made a new friend.

When thunder rumbled, Bambi
hurried to his cozy thicket.
    As he nestled close to his mother, the
pitter-patter of rain lulled him to sleep.

Later, sunshine filled the sky again and
Bambi's mother decided it was time to show
him the meadow. He followed her excitedly.

The meadow was so open and green that Bambi
darted forward. But his mother leaped in front of him.
"There may be danger!" she scolded.
Once she was sure it was safe, Bambi bounded into
the field and frolicked through the grass.

Suddenly, Bambi heard a *rrribit!*
It was a frog!
Bambi followed the frog until it
splashed into a nearby pond.

As Bambi gazed into the pond, he noticed his own reflection and the reflection of a smiling girl fawn.

Bambi ran back to his mother and hid between her legs.

"Kind of bashful, isn't he?" the girl fawn said.

"That's little Faline," Bambi's mother told him. "Go on. Say hello."

"Hello," he said shyly.

Faline giggled and began to chase him.
Bambi joined in the game and they played
happily in the field. Bambi had found a
new friend.

Then, a thundering herd of stags galloped
onto the meadow.
 The biggest stag stopped and looked at Bambi.
 Bambi asked his mother who the stag was.
 "He is very brave and wise," she answered.
"He is the Great Prince of the Forest."
 He was also Bambi's father.

Suddenly a gunshot sounded! The animals
panicked and scattered. In all the confusion,
Bambi lost his mother.

Instantly, the Great Prince was at Bambi's side.

He reunited Bambi with his mother and led them home safely.

Time passed quickly in the forest, and Bambi woke one morning to find the world covered in a soft white blanket. It was Bambi's first winter!

Bambi found Thumper skating on
the frozen pond.
"Come on, Bambi!" Thumper called.
It looked like so much fun!

Bambi ran toward the ice. With a *splat*, Bambi
slipped onto his belly, making Thumper giggle.
And when Thumper tried to teach him how
to balance on the ice, Bambi slid them both into
a snowbank!

They landed by a small, cozy den where Flower
lay sleeping. Flower explained that skunks hibernate,
so he would be sleeping all through the winter.
"Good night," he murmured, yawning.

The snowy days seemed endless,
and food grew scarce.

"I'm hungry, Mother," said Bambi.

"Winter won't last forever," she
assured him.

Finally, Bambi saw the first sign
of spring—a small patch of grass.
Bambi was nibbling at it when
a gunshot rang out!

Bambi ran as fast as his legs could
carry him. Soon he reached the thicket.
"We made it, Mother!" Bambi said.
But she wasn't there. Then Bambi
heard a second gunshot.

Bambi stepped out of the thicket.
The forest was silent, and snow was
falling all around him.

"Mother!" he called. "Where are you?"

As Bambi cried, the Great Prince appeared before him.

"Your mother can't be with you anymore," he said gently. "Come with me, my son."

Together, Bambi and his father walked deeper into the forest.

It wasn't long before flowers began
to bloom and birds' songs filled the air.
Even Flower awakened from his long
winter's sleep. Spring had finally arrived!

During the winter, Bambi had grown into a handsome buck. And Thumper and Flower had both grown to their full sizes, too.

When Friend Owl saw them, he said, "It won't be long before you're twitterpated. Nearly everyone falls in love in the springtime."

The three friends declared that it would never happen to them!

But soon Flower met a pretty skunk,
and he happily walked off with her.
She even gave him a kiss!

Thumper came across a
lovely female bunny. When she
petted his ears, Thumper's foot
went *thump, thump, thump*.

Without his friends, Bambi was lonely.
He stopped to drink from a pond, and a familiar
face looked back at him in the reflection.
    "Don't you remember me?" asked a sweet voice.
"I'm Faline."
    Faline the fawn had grown into a beautiful doe.

Together, Bambi and Faline played in the
meadow just as they had the summer before.
Now Bambi understood what Friend Owl meant.
He had never felt so happy.

Suddenly an angry stag appeared.
"Help!" cried Faline as the stag tried
to force her to come with him.
    Bambi butted the stag with all
his strength.

The defeated stag limped away,
and from that day on, Bambi and
Faline were inseparable.

Bambi awoke one morning sensing danger.
Smoke was in the air, and he could see a fire
burning in the distance.

The Great Prince told him, "It is man.
We must go deep into the forest. Hurry!"

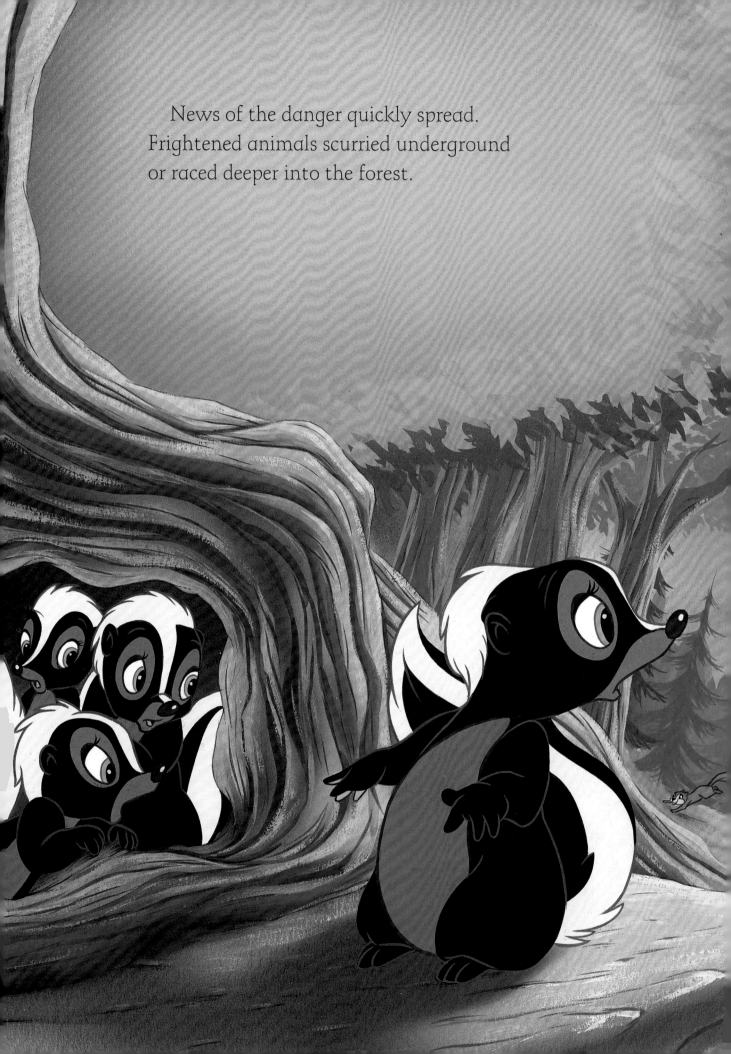

News of the danger quickly spread.
Frightened animals scurried underground
or raced deeper into the forest.

As Faline searched for Bambi, hunting dogs jumped at her from the bushes.

"Bambi!" she cried, scrambling to the top of a steep cliff.

The hounds snapped at her heels, barking. Faline was trapped!

Just then, Bambi sprang out of the woods and charged the dogs with his sharp antlers.

He attacked one dog after another until Faline bounded to safety.

Bambi escaped the dogs, but as he
leaped after Faline, a gunshot sounded.
Wounded, Bambi tumbled to the ground.
Fire raged toward him, but he couldn't
get up. Then he heard the voice of the
Great Prince.

"You must get up, Bambi,"
said the Great Prince.
Bambi staggered to his feet.
"Follow me," his father said.
"We'll be safe in the river."

Soon they came to a waterfall.
With nowhere else to turn, Bambi and
his father leaped toward the rapids below.

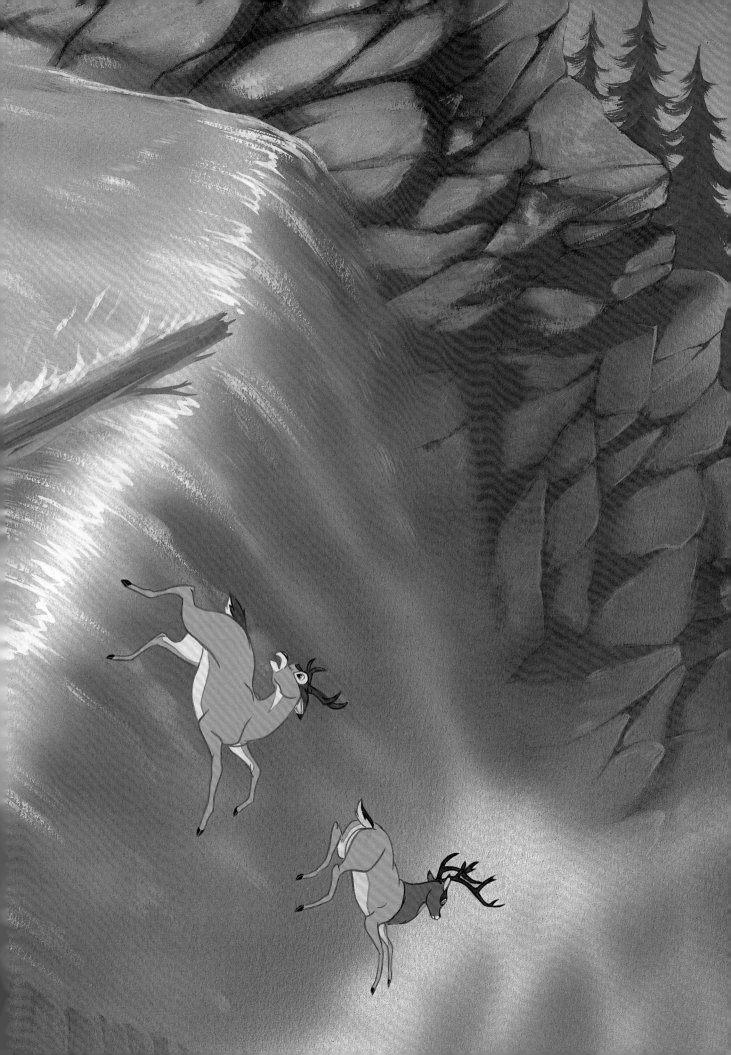

Bambi and the Great Prince finally reached the island, where Faline stood waiting. Even as they watched the beautiful forest burn, they all knew that when man was gone, the animals would bravely rebuild their homes.

Autumn turned to cold, white winter and then to spring.

"Wake up, Friend Owl!" cried Thumper and his four thumping baby bunnies.

"It's happened!" called Flower to the baby skunk scurrying behind him.

The animals gathered around the thicket
where Faline and her two fawns lay.

"Prince Bambi ought to be mighty proud,"
said the owl as the fawns opened their big
eyes to greet their friendly visitors.

Bambi was now the Prince of the Forest. And as he and his family began their lives together, Bambi thought of the lessons he hoped to teach his children—lessons he had learned from his mother and father long ago.

The End